Dana Wulfekotte

PEANUT
GETS
FED UP

Greenwillow Books, *An Imprint of* HarperCollins*Publishers*

For Jed (and Dolly)

Peanut Gets Fed Up. Copyright © 2022 by Dana Wulfekotte. All rights reserved. Manufactured in Italy. For information address HarperCollins Children's Books, a division of HarperCollins Publishers, 195 Broadway, New York, NY 10007. www.harpercollinschildrens.com

The art was done with pencil on paper and digitally colored in Adobe™ Photoshop™. The text type is Revival 555 BT.

Library of Congress Cataloging-in-Publication Data
Names: Wulfekotte, Dana, author.
Title: Peanut gets fed up / by Dana Wulfekotte.
Description: First edition. | New York : Greenwillow Books, An Imprint of HarperCollinsPublishers, [2022] | Audience: Ages 4-8 | Audience: Grades K-1 | Summary: "Peanut the stuffed penguin does everything with Pearl—napping and playing but also getting drooled on and dragged around. One day, Peanut has had enough. What happens when a stuffed animal ventures out on its own?"—Provided by publisher.
Identifiers: LCCN 2021039322 | ISBN 9780062455826 (hardback)
Subjects: CYAC: Toys—Fiction. | Friendship—Fiction.
Classification: LCC PZ7.1.W94 Pe 2022 | DDC [E]—dc23   LC record available at https://lccn.loc.gov/2021039322

22 23 24 25 26 RTLO 10 9 8 7 6 5 4 3 2 1 First Edition   Greenwillow Books

WELCOME HOME, PEARL!

Pearl and I have been together for a very long time.

We were together when she took her first steps.

And we were together when she said her first word.

But being together is not always fun.

Like during naptime,

or on rainy days,

or when the dog wants to play.

That's it!
I have had enough.

It is time
to take action.

Every Saturday morning, Pearl and I go to the park.

But today,

I won't be coming home.

Today I won't get dragged around

or drooled on or squished!

I can eat whatever I like.

And go wherever I want,

on my own,

without any help at all.

It feels great
to be free!

I certainly don't miss Pearl at all.

Look at that poor dog,
stuck on her leash.

Sure, she seems happy.
But if you look carefully, you can
tell she's planning her escape.

It's very obvious.

I wonder what Pearl
is doing right now.

I bet she's already
replaced me.

She probably hasn't even noticed that I ran away.

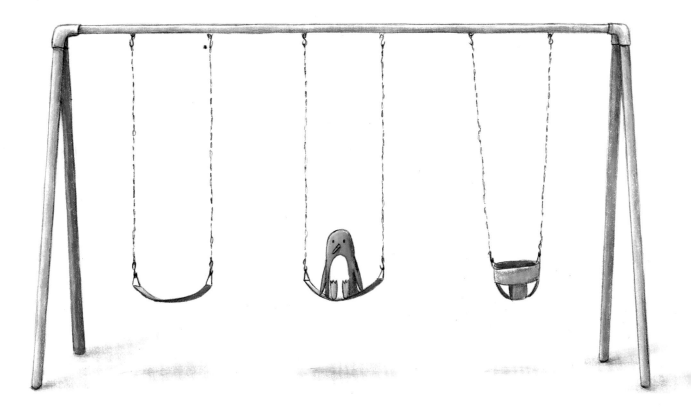

How can I swing
without anyone to push—

RIP

Oh no.

It can be easy to get fed up with someone when you've been stuck with them for so long.

But they're the ones who will always
be there to sew your stuffing back in. . . .

NO
DOGS!

Right when you need them.